The Boxcar Children investigate legendary creatures

The hike led the Aldens up and down hills, over mossy logs, and across streams. The ground in the rain forest was slippery with mud and fallen leaves.

"Are we almost there?" Jessie asked.

"We're very close now," said their guide, Nigel. He pointed to a hill across the clearing. At its base was a large, dark opening.

"Wow, is that a cave?" Benny asked.

"A tunnel," said Nigel.

"It looks like the tunnels that machines make," Henry said when they got close enough to get a good look.

"Except there were never any machines out here," Nigel said. "We believe an animal made this. A big animal."

Violet looked into the dark opening. "Is it still in there?"

THE BOXCAR CHILDREN®

CREATED BY
GERTRUDE CHANDLER WARNER

BOOK 4

MYTH OF THE RAIN FOREST MONSTER

STORY BY DEE GARRETSON

ALBERT WHITMAN & COMPANY
CHICAGO, ILLINOIS

CONTENTS

CHAPTER 1

CONCRETE JUNGLE

I don't see any rain forest." Six-year-old Benny Alden pressed his face against the car window. Outside, the streets were lined with buildings so tall Benny could not see the tops. The only trees in sight were palms, growing along the sidewalk.

"We've still got a long way to go before we get to the rain forest," Benny's older brother, Henry, said from the next row of the taxi van.

"That's right," said Dr. Iris. "Brazil is a very large

1

country. São Paulo is almost as far away from where we are going as Greenfield is from Camp Quest, where we met. But this place is an important stop for our next investigation."

"It is? Are we looking for a creature that lives in the city?" Benny looked back out the window and searched for any sign of wildlife.

Over the summer, he had gotten used to keeping his eye out for unusual things. He and his siblings were helping Dr. Iris investigate reports of mysterious creatures around the world. Their findings would help her prepare a television series for children. So far, the Aldens had looked for Bigfoot in the Rocky Mountains, elves in Iceland, and mermaids in Puerto Rico. Brazil was the last stop in the children's summer of travel. And Benny was determined to find the best proof yet that the creature was real—whatever it was.

"You won't see it in the streets, I'm afraid," Dr. Iris said. "We're actually going to the zoo."

Benny's eyes got big. "The creature is at the zoo?"

"That wouldn't be much of a mystery, would it?"

2

Henry chuckled and put down a map of the city. At fourteen, he was the oldest of the Alden children. He had been helping Dr. Iris navigate the busy city, and he was the only other one who knew what they were going to see.

"I love zoos," said Violet. "But aren't we going to see lots of the animals in the rain forest, where they live?"

Dr. Iris nodded. "We will see many animals there," she said. "But it can be hard to spot animals in the Amazon. And there's one animal in particular that is good at hiding in plain sight. It just so happens to have some things in common with the creature we'll be looking for."

"Sounds like a sneaky animal," said Benny. He bounced in his seat with excitement.

Violet wrung her hands. She was ten, and even though she was excited to be going to the rain forest, she also knew how wild it could be.

The taxi dropped off the children with Dr. Iris at the zoo. Once everyone had their tickets, the group walked inside. Immediately, they were surrounded by trees and vines and bright flowers.

"It's like stepping into a different world," said Jessie. She was twelve. Usually on the children's adventures, she was the planner. It was exciting for her not to know what they were going to do for a change.

Henry led them down a winding path through the zoo. Benny followed close behind, looking for a clue about what they were trying to find. They came to an enclosure of monkeys.

"Oh! Does the creature have really long arms and swing from the treetops?" Benny asked.

Dr. Iris shook her head. "We aren't here to see the monkeys."

Next, they passed an enclosure with a pair of yellow-and-blue birds.

"I know!" said Benny. "It's like a giant parrot with a big beak!"

One of the birds tilted its head from side to side.

Jessie laughed. "I don't think he liked you calling him a parrot, Benny." She pointed to the sign. "It says those are blue-and-yellow macaws."

"Oh." Benny turned to the enclosure. "Sorry, Mr. and Mrs. Macaw!"

"Just a little farther," said Henry.

He stopped at the end of the row and stood in front of the sign that said the name of the animal, so the others could not see. The enclosure had a grove of low-growing trees that shaded the whole area. Everyone gathered around and peered in. Even Jessie was excited to find what they were looking for.

Benny leaned on the railing. "I don't see anything in there. Are we looking for an invisible animal?"

Dr. Iris gave them a hint. "Look closely at the trees."

The children squinted as they scanned the treetops. Then Violet noticed something move among the leaves, and her eyes widened in surprise. "I see it!"

"I do too," Jessie said. "It just barely moved." She pointed up to an animal hanging from a branch. "See, Benny?"

"Yes!" Benny said. "It looks like a big monkey."

"Except its face is different," Violet said. She thought it looked kind of cute and was happy the animal they had come to see was not scary.

"That would be a sloth," said Dr. Iris. "Sloths are a little like monkeys. Both live in trees. But they move in very different ways."

Benny looked back at the monkey enclosure. One monkey climbed to the top of a tree in a blink. Another took a giant leap from one treetop to the next. Benny turned back to the sloth. "I think Mr. Sloth must be tired," he said. "Maybe he just woke up."

"Even when they are wide-awake, they don't jump like monkeys," Dr. Iris said. "Sloths sleep most of the time, so they don't have to spend as much energy looking for food as monkeys do."

"I like sleeping," said Benny. "But I thought the animal was going to be more…exciting."

"Well, sloths may not move fast," said Dr. Iris. "But that does not mean they aren't exciting. Moving slowly helps sloths stay hidden from predators. In fact,

they move so slowly that green algae grows in their fur. That makes them almost impossible to see in the green forest. So sloths may be slow, but they are masters of survival."

Benny looked up at the sloth. Staying hidden from other animals did sound exciting. "Sorry, Mr. Sloth," Benny said. "I didn't know you were a master survivor."

Jessie turned to Dr. Iris. "You said the animal would have something in common with the creature we'll be looking for. Is the creature good at staying hidden?"

"Or is it really slow and cute?" Violet asked.

Dr. Iris shook her head. "The creature we're here to learn about is sometimes said to be related to tree sloths. But it is much, much bigger. And it doesn't live in trees. It's called a mapinguary."

"Ma-ping-wahr-EE." Benny repeated the word part by part. "Does it have something to do with maps?"

"That's a good guess," Dr. Iris said. "No one is quite sure where the name comes from. You see, there are several languages spoken in the Amazon, including some that aren't very well-known to outsiders. What we do know is that many groups living around the Amazon have stories of this creature."

Another sloth emerged from the treetops. The children watched as it slowly climbed its way toward the other sloth on the branch.

"It's hard to think of a scary sloth," Benny said. He turned back to the enclosure. "No offense, Mr. and Mrs. Sloth."

Dr. Iris smiled. "Our next stop might help you imagine it more clearly. Where are we headed, Henry?"

"A natural history museum," said Henry, taking the city map back out. "That's where we'll see the skeleton."

"Skeleton!" said Violet. She remembered back to when they had been looking for Bigfoot. Dr. Iris had told them that they needed a real bone to show that the creature could be real. "Does that mean the creature is real?"

"Not necessarily," said Dr. Iris. "We're going to see a very old relative of the tree sloth—a giant ground sloth."

"There are sloths that live on the ground too?" said Benny.

Dr. Iris shook her head. "Most people believe that the last giant sloths went extinct thousands of years ago. But some say the creature is still alive and that it is actually what the stories of the mapinguary are talking about."

Jessie took out her notepad and pen. "So we've got three different questions to answer," she said. "The first question is about this creature, the mapinguary: Is it real? The second is about this animal: Are there still giant ground sloths alive in the Amazon? And the third question is whether the mapinguary and the ground sloth are the same thing."

Dr. Iris nodded. "Perfectly stated, Jessie! That is just how we should open this episode of the television show. Now, we should be on our way."

As the Aldens were leaving the zoo, another

animal caught Benny's eye. The creature walked on all four legs and had a long snout. "What is this guy's name?" Benny asked. "His nose is like an elephant's."

The others stopped and looked in the enclosure. Violet read the sign. "It says here that it's a giant anteater," she said. "It lives in the Amazon too." She read off the extra information about the animal. "It can eat thirty thousand insects a day! Its snout helps scoop them up."

Benny watched as the animal snuffled its nose along the ground. "So far we've seen one animal that likes to sleep *a lot*," he said. "And another one that likes to eat *a lot*. I think I want to live in the Amazon too."

Dr. Iris chuckled. "It is not so easy for humans," she said. "The anteater has had a long time to adapt, just like the sloth."

"What do you mean?" Henry asked.

"The Amazon is unlike any other place on Earth," Dr. Iris said. "Every animal in the rain forest has changed over time so it can live in the rain forest's unique conditions. The anteater has found a way to take advantage of all the insects in the forest. His snout makes him a master at scooping them up."

"Like how the sloth adapted to become a master of disguise," said Jessie.

"Correct again!" said Dr. Iris. "Now, let's move along. I don't want to be late for our next appointment."

As the rest of the group headed toward the exit, Jessie paused to write on her notepad. Their conversation seemed like an important thing to remember.

"Come on, Ms. Sloth!" Benny called back to her.

Jessie laughed. She closed her notepad and ran to catch up.

CHAPTER 2

A MEGA CLUE

L ook!" Violet said. "That building has a mural painted on it. And there's another one on that building! The flowers on it are pretty."

"There's one with monkeys!" Benny said. "They're everywhere!"

"São Paulo is famous for its street art," Dr. Iris said. "The artwork reminds everyone of the country's most fabulous treasure."

"They have a treasure?" Benny asked. "What

kind of treasure?"

"The rain forest is Brazil's greatest treasure," Dr. Iris answered. "Really, it's a treasure for everyone on Earth. But we'll have to talk about that later. We're here!"

The taxi let everyone out in front of a white stone building. "What does that sign say?" Violet asked. "I can't read any of those words."

"I am not surprised!" said Dr. Iris. "It's written in Portuguese, the official language of Brazil."

"'Museu de Zoologia da Universidade de São Paulo,'" Henry read off the words slowly. "I think I know what that means. The words almost look like Spanish: Museum of Zoology at the University of São Paulo."

"That's right. Portuguese and Spanish are alike in some ways," Dr. Iris said. "But most people in Brazil do not speak Spanish. Lucky for us, the man we are meeting is an old friend, and he speaks English."

A man wearing a bow tie and a white suit came through the door of the museum.

"Hello!" Dr. Iris called.

"Welcome, Iris," the man said as he came over to her. "It's been too long." He kissed her on both cheeks.

"This is Professor Cardoso," Dr. Iris said to the Aldens. The man had white hair and dark-brown eyes. "He's an expert on animal species in the Amazon." She introduced each of the children.

"I'm so pleased to meet you," he said to them. However, as the man shook each of their hands, his eyebrows wrinkled. Violet thought he looked worried.

Professor Cardoso turned to Dr. Iris. "You didn't mention the age of your young companions." He looked down at Benny. "Camping in the Amazon can be dangerous. There are enough animals, reptiles, and insects to cause problems for the most experienced of campers."

"We've been on lots of adventures!" Benny said. He raised his arm and flexed his muscles.

"So Iris has told me." The professor gave a friendly smile, but Violet still thought he looked worried.

"Nigel Livingstone will be along with us," Dr. Iris said. "I haven't met him, but I know he's an expert."

"I was surprised to hear you were traveling with Nigel," the professor said. "I thought he'd given up on those trips after the attack."

"Attack?" Violet asked.

"Yes, he had an unfortunate run-in with a caiman," said the professor. "Last I heard, he still walks with a limp."

"Oh dear, I didn't know about that," said Dr. Iris. "He seemed excited to go on the expedition in his emails. He never mentioned any trouble."

"A caiman?" Henry asked. "That's like an alligator, isn't it?"

Professor Cardoso nodded. "They are very similar to alligators. Except they don't grow as large."

"Why did a caiman bite him?" Benny asked. "Did it sneak up on him at night?"

"No, caiman don't do that," Professor Cardoso said. "He said he just wasn't paying close enough attention. Caiman don't usually attack humans, though it's best to stay out of their way."

"We are always careful," Dr. Iris said with a bright

smile. "Now, why don't we have a look inside? Thank you for opening the museum for us."

"Of course," Professor Cardoso said. "This way."

———

"*That's* what we are looking for?" said Benny.

The skeleton was in the center of a large hall, and it stood at least three times as tall as Professor Cardoso. The creature's two front legs grasped a thick tree. Its back legs were planted on the ground with a sturdy-looking tail between them. The children walked around the skeleton. It was as big as some of the dinosaurs they had seen at other museums.

"There were once more than twenty species of giant ground sloths, including some that lived in North America," Professor Cardoso said. "The species that lived here in South America was the largest though. It's called the Megatherium. That means *giant beast*. We think it weighed about seven tons."

Jessie did the math out loud. "If one ton is two

thousand pounds, that means it weighed fourteen thousand pounds!"

"That sounds like a lot," Benny said.

The professor nodded. "It weighed about as much as a *Tyrannosaurus rex*. Or you can think of it another way: if you stacked four cars on top of each other, the stack would weigh about the same amount."

Benny nodded. "Definitely a lot."

"I'm not sure I want to go looking for something that big," said Violet. "Plus, the front claws are scary looking."

"We don't think ground sloths were dangerous to humans," Professor Cardoso said. "They were herbivores. That means they only ate plants."

"How do scientists know that?" asked Violet.

"Good question," Professor Cardoso said. "The skeletons include jaws and teeth. Teeth tell us quite a bit about an animal. I know it's hard to see the teeth in this one because it's so tall, but we have photographs on the display."

The professor pointed at one of the images. "See

how the teeth are flat? If the animals had eaten meat, they'd need some sharper teeth in front. They don't have any pointed or sharp teeth. That tells us they ate plants."

"Dr. Iris said that some people think there could be an animal like this still out there," said Henry. "It's odd to think that no one has seen or photographed something so big."

"That's right," said Professor Cardoso. "I don't believe any of these creatures are still alive. Our evidence points to this type of animal going extinct nine or ten thousand years ago. But your guide, Nigel, has his own theory."

"We should look for evidence," Dr. Iris reminded the children. "But we can't forget that we don't know everything. Remember when we were learning about mermaids, we talked about a fish that was thought to have been extinct, but people found one alive quite recently."

Jessie nodded, but she couldn't remember the fish's name.

"Ah, yes, the coelacanth," Professor Cardoso said. "Unfortunately, we know even less about the ocean than we do about the rain forest. But, on the other hand, dozens of new species are found every year in the Amazon. I suppose there's no harm in investigating what is the cause of all of these stories."

Henry turned back to the skeleton. "Why do you think these sloths went extinct?" he asked.

"We don't know for sure, but we think it's because, sadly, humans hunted them into extinction," the professor explained. "Unlike dinosaurs, giant ground sloths were alive at the same time as humans. And because humans hunted together, the sloths' size was not enough to protect them. Overhunting has been the cause of many animals' extinctions, especially megafauna."

"Mega-what?" asked Benny.

"Megafauna," the professor said, leading them around the rest of the hall. "Those were the very large animals."

"That's terrible," Violet said. "I don't want any animals to disappear forever."

"Back then, people didn't think about conservation," said Dr. Iris. "Even today, there are many animals that may go extinct from too much hunting. As we discover new animals, we are losing others."

Professor Cardoso stopped at what looked like a skeleton of a giant armadillo. "It isn't just animals either. Plants and habitats are in danger too. We lose more every year."

"I don't understand," Jessie said. "How can you lose part of the Amazon?"

"I should say they are taken, not lost," the professor said. "Some trees in the rain forest are very rare. There are laws protecting them, but there are illegal loggers who will take whatever trees they want. I've seen how Nigel acts when he runs across these loggers. He'll try to chase them away all by himself."

"He sounds brave," Henry said.

"He's brave about most things, but not everything."

Professor Cardoso chuckled. "I'll tell you a little secret. I expect he's going to show you the scar on his head. He shows it to everyone. That's why he shaves his head. He's going to tell you a jaguar tried to bite him, but I know the truth. The truth is that he cut himself with his own machete on accident. A tarantula fell onto his head and surprised him. He has a terrible fear of spiders, even after all these years working in the Amazon. He forgot he had such a big knife in his hand and nicked himself trying to shoo it away!"

"Oh dear," Dr. Iris said. "He could have really hurt himself."

"I don't like spiders either," Violet said. "I don't know if I'll ever get used to them."

Professor Cardoso snapped his fingers. "That reminds me, I have a gift for each of you to bring on your adventure. Let's go back to my office for a moment."

When they reached the professor's office, he took four books from a stack on his desk. "The Amazon has thousands of species. These guidebooks will help you identify what you see. The one on birds is written by your guide, Nigel."

Professor Cardoso gave Henry a book on animals and fish. To Jessie, he gave a book about plants. Violet got the book about birds, and Benny received a book about insects.

"I can't wait to keep track of everything," said Jessie. "Our grandfather will want to hear all about our trip."

"Speaking of James, he'd never forgive me if we missed your flight this evening," said Dr. Iris. "And we've got some sightseeing to do before then!"

The professor nodded. Then his eyebrow wrinkled once again. "Before you go. I do have a message for you to give to Nigel. You see, his son was supposed to contact me about an old story I used to tell, so he could make a recording of it. That boy of his could never get enough of scary stories, even when he was just a little boy. But I haven't heard from him, and I don't know why. I'm starting to get worried."

"Of course," said Dr. Iris. Then her phone made a dinging sound. "Excuse me, I should check this." She pulled the phone from her pocket. "It's a text message from Nigel. That's strange. The message says, 'Hurry! Possible sighting!'"

"It looks like there's an audio message attached," said Jessie.

Dr. Iris pushed play on the recording. For a moment it was quiet. There was only a low rumbling on the other end of the line. Then the noise grew from a rumble to a growl.

Suddenly the growl turned to a roar. It was so loud Dr. Iris dropped her phone onto the desk in surprise.

The sound of running footsteps came from the phone's speaker. Then the recording ended.

STORIES FROM
THE FOREST

Violet shuddered. "Do you think that was the mapinguary?"

Henry picked up the phone from the desk and handed it back to Dr. Iris. "Professor Cardoso, did you recognize that sound?" he asked. "Is it an animal you know of in the Amazon?"

"Play it again, please," he said.

After Dr. Iris played it a second time, Professor

Cardoso shook his head. "It's very poor quality. The noise could be anything, even a loud engine. I can't pinpoint a particular animal from that."

"I'll text Nigel back and ask him where he got it. He must know we need more information about a possible piece of evidence like this." Dr. Iris sent the message. The phone dinged again almost right away. She looked at it and sighed. "He didn't answer the question. He just says, 'Get here today.' I suppose we can leave for Manaus early if it will help with the investigation, but I'll need to make some phone calls."

The children explored the museum while Dr. Iris made the arrangements. After they had toured all the rooms, they went back to look at the giant sloth skeleton one more time.

"This is scarier than the other creatures we've learned about," Violet said. She moved around to the back of the skeleton so she didn't have to look at its long claws.

"Don't worry, Violet," Jessie said. "We'd hear something like this crashing through the forest."

"That's right!" Benny said. He stomped around in a circle with his arms outstretched. "It would make a lot of noise."

"We don't even know if the mapinguary is real or if giant sloths still exist," Henry reminded them.

Benny stopped moving. "But that man who is in the Amazon, Mr. Livingstone, thinks it's real," he said.

"I'm sure if Nigel is a real scientist, he knows he can't say it's real unless he can prove it," Jessie said. "Remember what Dr. Iris taught us."

"Always follow the evidence," said Violet.

Dr. Iris and Professor Cardoso came into the room. "And that is just what we will do," she said. "But first, we have a plane to catch."

———

It was a rush to get through the airport and onto the plane to Manaus, but the children climbed aboard just as the doors were closing.

Once they were settled, Jessie pulled out her

guidebook on plants. "It was nice of the professor to give these to us," she said.

"Very nice," Dr. Iris agreed. "I'm glad he thought of it. The Amazon is fascinating even without the stories about the mapinguary."

"Do you think that was a real recording of the creature?" Henry asked her.

"I don't know. One audio file doesn't prove anything, especially since we don't know where it was recorded. But there are many stories about the mapinguary where we are going. Unlike São Paulo, Manaus is a city close to the rain forest. We may be able to start getting some real clues very soon."

As soon as the plane landed and the children stepped off the stairs onto the tarmac, the heat hit them. Jessie used her guidebook to fan her face. "I don't think we're going to need the heavier clothes we brought."

"Believe it or not, it can get cold at night in the rain forest," Dr. Iris said. "I was very thorough with our packing list. We will have just what we need for our excursion. Now, once we collect our luggage, we'll find a taxi to take us to our boat."

"We get to take a boat?" said Benny. "Yay!"

Dr. Iris nodded. "There are very few roads in the Amazon," she explained. "In fact, it would have been difficult to get to this city by road. Roads through the jungle are difficult to maintain. Plants here grow so fast they'd cover up the road in no time."

Outside the airport, Dr. Iris hailed a taxi, and the driver helped them load their luggage. Henry sat in front with the driver. The man spoke English well, and he was very interested in why they were visiting Manaus.

Henry explained about their travels and about Dr. Iris's television show. "We're here to investigate the mapinguary," he said finally. "Have you heard of it?"

At the name of the creature, the driver pulled over to the side of the road, and the car screeched to a stop.

"Look over there," the man said, pointing out the window. The taxi had stopped on the edge of a plaza. Along one side, a mural filled a wall of a building. In front of the mural stood an array of statues.

"There, at the end," the man said. "There is a statue of the mapinguary."

"Can we get out and look at it?" Jessie asked.

The taxi driver nodded, and Dr. Iris opened her door. "Yes, let's see what people believe it looks like."

The children walked across the plaza toward the statue. As they got closer, Violet thought it looked even scarier than the skeleton they had seen. "It's like a big gorilla standing up on its back legs," she said. "Except it has really long claws!"

Benny pointed at the creature's forehead, where there was a single eye. "Why does it only have one eye? That's creepy."

"Very creepy," Violet agreed. "And what is that awful thing on its stomach?"

The statue had an oval opening right below its chest. There were sharp, jagged teeth lining the opening.

"I think that is supposed to be a mouth," Jessie said.

"That's horrible!" Violet cried. "I'd rather find a

giant sloth than this thing. It really is a monster!"

Jessie turned to Dr. Iris. "Does any real creature have just one eye?" she asked. "I can't think of one."

"That is a very good question," Dr. Iris said. "There is only one tiny sea creature that I know of with only one eye. It's called a copepod. Most creatures have something called bilateral symmetry."

"What does that mean?" said Benny.

"It means they have one line that divides them into two mirror images." She moved over to a mural that had a giant butterfly on it, next to the statue. "Like this butterfly. If you drew a line from its head to its tail, the two halves would be the same. It would be very strange to see an animal with a single eye in the center of its head."

"But people have said they've seen a monster like this," Benny said. "Why would they make it up?"

"I've heard of a one-eyed monster in stories," Henry said. "It's called a cyclops. People believed that creature was real for a long time."

"Maybe they created it to scare people," said

Jessie. "We are afraid of things that are strange. And something with one eye and a mouth on its stomach is definitely strange!"

Back in the taxi, Henry asked the driver, "Do you know anyone who has ever seen the mapinguary?"

"No, but people tell many stories about it," the man said. "Some people say it is the protector of the forest. If someone cuts down trees they shouldn't or traps an animal, they say the mapinguary will get revenge." Then the driver laughed. "My mother used to tell me not to go outside at night because the mapinguary might get me. It worked to keep me inside!"

The man started the car back up, and they were back on their way.

Jessie took out her notepad. The driver's story about the mapinguary seemed like another important thing to remember.

They drove down streets lined with buildings painted in pink and yellow and blue. Street vendors on the sidewalks called out to passersby, selling food and souvenirs from their stands and carts.

"This is a busy place," Violet said.

"Manaus is the largest city in the Amazon region, and for people traveling up the river, it's often the best place to start their trips," the taxi driver said as he let them off at a large dock area. He pointed to the right. "Most of the passenger boats are that way. You shouldn't have any trouble finding yours. They all have names painted on them. Have a good trip, but don't let any mapinguaries get you!" He smiled and waved as he drove away.

The docks were crowded with boats, most of them with two or three decks.

"What kind of boats are these?" Violet asked. "They look like houseboats, except bigger."

"They are called riverboats," Dr. Iris explained. "Since it takes a long time to get places on the river, it's easier if you go on a boat you can live on. There are very few places to stay on the shore. We need to find a riverboat called the *Toucan*. The captain's name is Paolo Souza."

They read the names on each boat as they walked.

"I don't see it," Dr. Iris said when they were almost at the end.

"Here it is," Violet said.

She stopped in front of a small, wooden riverboat tucked between two larger boats. It leaned to one side, and part of the railing around the lower deck was missing. Barrels had been stacked to block the gap. The name of the boat, *Toucan*, was painted on it in faded letters.

Henry looked at the boat doubtfully. "How far is this boat supposed to take us?"

CHAPTER 4

VISITORS

"T his is not what I had in mind when I told Nigel to organize a boat for us," Dr. Iris said. "Hello!" she called out.

A yipping sound answered from the top of the boat.

"That sounds like a little dog," said Benny.

"Maybe the captain has a pet. Hello!" Dr. Iris called again. A man in a bright-orange shirt and a straw hat appeared on the top deck.

"I'm Iris Perez," Dr. Iris called up to him. "We're here to meet Nigel Livingstone. Are you Captain Souza?"

"I am! Come aboard." The man came down the steps to greet them.

Once they were on board, Dr. Iris introduced everyone. Then she asked, "Where is Nigel?"

"He didn't tell you?" the captain said. "Nigel has gone upriver in a pair of small boats with his guide. They are going to check out a report of a mapinguary sighting. Then he's going on to the camp, so you'll meet up with him there. Are you ready to go?"

"Now? I thought we'd leave in the morning," Dr. Iris said. "I wanted to check over all the supplies Nigel was supposed to get for us."

The captain frowned. "I'm afraid that won't work. He told me you'd be ready to go as soon as you arrived in Manaus. I need to get upriver today."

"Oh dear. Did he leave the supplies with you? I don't think everything would fit on whatever small boats he has."

Captain Souza nodded. "He had a bunch of things loaded up yesterday. You can go take a look if you want. They're in Cabin Two. But I'd like to get started to keep on schedule."

Dr. Iris hesitated for a moment. Like Jessie, Dr. Iris liked to have everything in order before setting out. Jessie could tell she was not happy about all of the changes in plan.

"All right, we'll have to trust that he got everything on my list," Dr. Iris said. "After all, he's the expert. We can leave."

The captain laughed. "I'm not sure I'd call Nigel an expert, but from the amount of gear he loaded up, you should have more than enough supplies."

"He's written a guidebook about the birds of the Amazon," Jessie said. "Doesn't that make him an expert?"

"I don't know about any book," Captain Souza said. "He's a very confident fellow. I'll say that for him. Now, let's get all your luggage aboard."

Captain Souza helped the Aldens carry their

suitcases up the boarding ramp. "You can have Cabin One and Three to sleep in tonight," he said. "But first, can I have a hand untying the ropes from the dock? I've only got two other crew members aboard, and one is down in the galley working on dinner. The other is sleeping before he takes the night watch."

"Sure," Henry said.

"We'll be glad to help," Jessie added.

The captain went back up to the pilothouse, calling down to them with instructions. Henry and Jessie untied the boat and then stood at the railing as the boat pulled away from the dock. Soon the boat was around a bend, and the city had disappeared from view.

"Let's check out those supplies," Dr. Iris said.

Cabin Two had a jumble of equipment and supplies piled on the bunks and floor. In some places the boxes were stacked to the ceiling.

"This is a lot of stuff," Benny said.

"It looks like someone was in a hurry to get all of it in here," added Henry. "They didn't even try to organize it."

Violet picked up a package that held some plastic paddles and a net. "I think this is a table tennis set."

Dr. Iris scratched her head. "I certainly didn't put that on the list."

"Maybe the creature likes to play games!" said Benny.

Henry picked up a tipped-over box from the floor. "Wow, this one is full of night vision googles." He took a pair out and put them on.

Benny laughed. "You look like a giant bug!"

"That wasn't on my list either," Dr. Iris said. "I wasn't intending on walking around in the rain forest at night."

Jessie could tell Dr. Iris was getting concerned. "Why don't we organize the supplies," Jessie suggested. "That way we will know which ones were on the list and which are extra."

Dr. Iris nodded. "Good idea."

Together, the group began moving boxes around. They put the things that were on Dr. Iris's list on one side of the cabin and the things not on the list on the other side.

"This box has little cameras attached to straps," Jessie said.

"Yes, those were Nigel's idea. He wanted to film everything in case we saw the creature. The small cameras attach to vests, so we don't have to carry around a big camera."

Jessie placed the cameras in the pile of things that were on the list.

"Here's one full of hats," Violet said. "All different kinds."

Dr. Iris shook her head, and Violet put the box in the other pile.

Benny held up a small box. "There's a telephone here, but it looks a little like a walkie-talkie."

"That's a satellite phone," Dr. Iris said. "It's for camping in places where it's hard to get a signal. I hope there is a box of boots. I gave him a list of all your sizes."

"They're here," Jessie said, holding up a pair. "Does it rain so much we need rain boots?"

Dr. Iris checked another box. "No, but we're

all going to need to wear boots any time we aren't sleeping to protect ourselves from snake bites and insect bites."

"Really?" Violet asked. "Is the camp going to be that dangerous?"

Dr. Iris gave a gentle smile. "No, it's just a precaution. It's always better to be careful."

They went through all the supplies, sorting and stacking them to make more room in the cabin. When they were done, there were two neat piles about the same size. "Everything is here," said Henry. "And a lot of extra things too. Nigel brought lots of electronics, like cameras and computers."

"I don't understand why Nigel has included some of this equipment, but I suppose he must have his reasons," said Dr. Iris. "He's been doing this a long time."

"Listen," Violet said. "I hear the yipping noise again."

The children were quiet for a moment. Sure enough, what sounded like the bark of a small puppy was coming from outside.

"We forgot to ask if the captain has a dog," said Benny. "Can we go see?"

"Yes, go ahead," Dr. Iris told them. "I want to make a phone call while I can still get a signal on my regular cell phone."

It was getting dark when the Aldens climbed the stairs to the top deck.

"Over here," Henry said. "I think that little room at the front of the boat is called the pilothouse. That's where the captain steers the boat."

Captain Souza was humming to himself when they walked in.

"We thought we heard a little dog," Violet said.

The captain laughed. Without taking his eyes off the river, he pointed to the corner of the pilothouse. "You're hearing my pal, Figly."

Instead of a dog, a large, black bird with a long, orange beak sat on a perch at the back of the pilothouse. Each of its eyes had a blue circle of tiny feathers around it.

"That's a toucan, isn't it?" Jessie asked.

"It certainly is," the captain said.

"He's so colorful," said Violet. "And his call is so unique."

"Yes, the toucan is very good at standing out," said the captain. "And it needs to be."

"Why?" asked Benny.

"With so many frogs and birds and insects making noise in the Amazon, and with so much land, toucans need to be able to find each other. They do that through their colors and with their calls."

Jessie thought back to their visit to the zoo. "It reminds me of how the sloth has changed over time to fit in. Except the toucan seems to have adapted to stand out."

The bird turned to the children and gave a dog-like yip. Violet noticed one of its wings looked different from the other. "Did something happen to him?" she asked.

"Yes, his wing was injured when he was a chick. That's why I have him. He couldn't take care of himself. You can feed him a treat if you want."

The captain pointed to a little bowl of treats. "Take one and hold it out for him. He likes figs. That's why I named him Figly."

Benny grabbed a treat and held it out. In a flash, the toucan's long beak grabbed the treat and gobbled it up, flinging bits everywhere. Benny laughed.

"They're messy eaters," Captain Souza chuckled. "I get used to having bits of fruit in my hair."

The bird gave one more yip and then hopped to the floor. "Better move back so he can get out. Toucans don't sit still for very long. He likes to roam around the decks."

The Aldens made a path for the bird. He hopped between them and then out the door, making his yipping call as he went.

When they turned back, the captain was pointing to the shore. "Take a look over there."

It had gotten so dark that they could just make out the shapes of some large creatures sliding into the water.

"Those are caiman, aren't they?" Jessie said.

"Yes, the particular species you see along here are black caiman. They are very hard to see once they're in the water, even in daylight. They blend right in."

"We heard they can be dangerous," Violet said.

"Yes, a man we met said Nigel had been bitten by one," Benny added. "I don't see them anymore. Are they following us?"

"No, no," the captain said. "Caiman usually don't bother people unless people bother them. The river is their world. We are just visitors. I hadn't heard that about Nigel though."

Jessie thought it was strange that Nigel hadn't told Captain Souza about his caiman attack. It seemed like it had been a big deal for him. But before she could ask anything more about it, a noise came from up ahead. It sounded like the hum of an engine.

Captain Souza's expression turned serious. He turned on a bright spotlight. "This, however, might be trouble."

CHAPTER 5

INTO THE WILD

The riverboat's light shone down on a speedboat with one man in it. The man waved as he turned his boat to go around the *Toucan*.

Captain Souza waved back and let out a big sigh. "That's a relief," he said. "I was afraid it would be a river-pirate boat. We don't usually get river pirates on this part of the river, but I don't like hearing the sound of a small boat at night. Most people don't travel in those sorts of boats after dark, except for pirates."

"There are really pirates here?" Henry asked.

"I thought they were just in stories about the olden days," Violet said.

"Sadly, there are still pirates," the captain said. "They don't wear eye patches or have peg legs, but they can be dangerous. In such a remote area, pirates think they can take what they want from anyone."

"It reminds me of the loggers who cut down trees illegally," said Jessie.

Captain Souza nodded. "That's right. Sometimes it's not the animals who pose the most danger in the Amazon; it's the humans."

"I think I hear something rumbling," Benny said. "Is there another boat coming?"

The captain laughed. He checked his watch. "That was my stomach! It's almost time for dinner. I'll join you in the main room on the lower deck in a few minutes. Once we lower the table down, we can eat."

"What do you mean?" Henry asked.

The captain smiled. "Go look."

The children went downstairs to the main room.

It did not look like a dining room. "Are we sure this is the right place?"

Then Jessie pointed to the ceiling. "The table is up there!"

Sure enough, there was a chain holding the table near the ceiling.

"I've never seen a table on a ceiling before," Violet said. "Why would it be up there?"

"We make use of all the space we can on riverboats," the captain explained as he came into the room. "If we have a lot of passengers, we lift the table up at night so we can string hammocks in this room for people to sleep." He pointed at some hooks in the walls. "See, we can fit a dozen hammocks in here if we need to. You should be glad you have cabins though. It can get loud at night if one person is snoring."

Jessie, Violet, and Benny looked at Henry.

"Hey, I don't snore!" he said.

"Oh, yes you do," Dr. Iris said as she walked into the room. The children laughed.

Once the table was down and the folding chairs

were in place, everyone sat down. Dinner was a fish and vegetable stew served over rice. For dessert, they had Brazilian treats that the captain called *brigadeiros*.

"It's a bit like a truffle," the captain said, passing the tray around. "I don't know exactly how it's made; I'm not much of a cook. I just know I like them!"

Benny ate one. "I don't care how they are made. These are delicious!"

The tray went around the table until the treats were all gone. After everyone was done eating, the Aldens helped clear the table and raise it back to the ceiling. Once that was finished, Henry looked at a map on the wall. "Which way are we going?" he asked.

The captain came over and traced his finger along a blue line. "We're going north. There aren't as many towns along this stretch." He pointed at a black dot. "I'm taking you here."

"Are all those blue lines rivers?" Violet asked. "I thought the Amazon was just one big river."

"Big rivers are often big because smaller rivers flow into them," the captain explained. "The

Amazon River has more than one thousand rivers and streams feeding into it. It's the largest river system in the world. In fact, we aren't even on the Amazon River right now. We are going up a river called the Rio Negro, which means 'black river.'"

"I saw that the water was very dark," said Violet. "Why is that?" Something about floating on a river with such murky water made her nervous.

"During the rainy season, much of this area floods," the captain explained. "Huge areas of plant life suddenly go underwater. As the plants break down, they give off the black color. Some people say the water looks like black tea."

After dinner, everyone went to the top deck, where the night pilot was steering the boat. Besides the lights on the *Toucan*, the only other light came from the moon shining on the water. Violet liked imagining they were floating on a river of tea. But the huge wilderness and the stories of the mapinguary still worried her.

"It feels like we are all alone out here," she said.

"It's like you said, Captain Souza; we are visitors here."

Captain Souza smiled. "We may be visitors," he said. "But I've learned that as long as we are good guests, everything will be fine."

That made Violet feel better. The Alden children knew how to be good guests. Before long, Violet was yawning along with Benny, and it was time to go to sleep.

———

"It feels early, even though the sun is already up," Benny said the next morning as they went to eat breakfast.

"It *is* early," Dr. Iris said. "The sun rises around six a.m. year-round along the equator. And that means daylight lasts almost exactly twelve hours. The sun sets at six p.m."

Jessie fanned herself. "It's already hot too."

"The equator is the part of Earth closest to the sun, so there are no cold winters here," Dr. Iris said.

"It only gets slightly cooler during the rainy season."

"I like it when it's hot," Benny said. He rubbed his stomach. "But I like cold breakfast. I wonder what we're having."

In the main room, breakfast was already waiting for them. There was granola and yogurt with bananas and berries.

"What kind of berries are these?" Jessie asked. "They look like blueberries, except they're a darker purple."

"Those are acai berries," Captain Souza said. "The Amazon has several different kinds of fruit you've probably never seen before."

"On the plane, I was reading the guidebook Professor Cardoso gave me about plants," Jessie said. "The book says there are more than eighty thousand different kinds of plants in the Amazon."

Dr. Iris nodded. "That's one reason why I said the Amazon was a treasure for the whole world."

Benny swallowed a big bite of yogurt and berries. "How can plants be treasure?" he asked.

"There are a couple ways," Dr. Iris explained.

"First, plants make oxygen, which is what us humans breathe. The Amazon has so many plants, people call it the lungs of the world. Also, many medicines we use today were first discovered from the plants that grow here."

"Not to mention plants are food for lots of animals," said Benny.

Dr. Iris chuckled. "That is true. I can always count on you to think of the most important thing, Benny—food!"

The trip up the river took all day. Every once in a while, the boat would pass a small village. At one village, a bright-yellow boat was parked at the dock.

"It looks like a school bus," Violet said.

"It *is* a school bus," Dr. Iris said. "Or I should say, a school boat. Many of the villages here are too small to have their own schools, so a school boat picks up the children to take them to a bigger village that does have a school."

Soon, there were no more villages, just forest on both sides of the river. The Aldens spent most of the time sitting on the deck, watching the shore and reading their guidebooks.

"I haven't seen many animals," Violet said. "It's too hard to see through the trees."

Jessie turned to her sister. "Look behind us."

"Dolphins!" said Violet. In the boat's wake, a pod of dolphins was swimming along and leaping out of the water.

"I thought dolphins lived in the ocean," said Benny. "Turn around, Mr. and Mrs. Dolphin!" he called. "You're going the wrong way!"

"Those are river dolphins, Benny." Henry held up his guidebook. "According to this, they're called botos. I hope they get close. The book says that some of them, the older ones, look pink."

The animals swam closer to the boat, like they wanted to follow it. Violet pointed. "There's a pink one—that big one!"

The smaller ones around it were mostly gray. The children watched as the dolphins swam around the *Toucan* curiously then swam off ahead.

It was late afternoon when the riverboat slowed and pulled up to a wooden pier. At the other end of the pier, a man with curly blond hair was jiggling a plastic object in front of him.

"What is that man doing?" Benny asked.

"It looks like he's holding a coffee maker," Jessie said. "But I don't know why he would be doing that."

"Hello! I'm Iris Perez," Dr. Iris called out. "We're looking for Nigel Livingstone. Have you seen him?"

The man stopped jiggling the object and stood up straight. "Nigel Livingstone, at your service."

"I thought he was supposed to have a shaved head," Violet said to her siblings.

Jessie shrugged. "I guess he decided to let his hair grow."

Captain Souza tied up the boat to the dock, and the man came out to meet them. Dr. Iris stepped off the boat. "You're Nigel Livingstone?" She sounded puzzled.

"Yes," the man said, looking over her shoulder at the boat. "Who else would I be?"

CHAPTER 6

BASE CAMP

The man held up his wallet, which contained a driver's license with a photo of the man smiling. Next to the photo was the man's name, Nigel Livingstone.

"Right," Dr. Iris said. "I'm sorry for my confusion. I didn't realize you were so young. You've accomplished quite a bit in your career."

Nigel shrugged. "I graduated from college early and jumped right in. Come on, I'll show you the camp." He looked down at the coffee maker. "I think it's got enough charge to work now."

"Is that a solar panel on top of the coffee maker?" Henry asked.

"Yes, it's the latest thing," Nigel said. "I like a good cup of coffee every morning, so I thought this would be perfect. Except the camp is too shady for it to get a good charge. I didn't think about that."

Two long boats that looked like canoes with motors attached were tied up to the dock. Benny knelt down to get a better look at them. "Are these boats made out of logs?" he asked.

"Yes," Nigel said. "Some of the small boats that people use to get up and down the river are still made the traditional way. Aren't they terrific? They look great on film too. Follow me, and I'll show you the camp."

Henry and Jessie looked at each other. Nigel did not seem like the person they had imagined.

He led the way up the riverbank. Ahead, a post stood with a board nailed to it. The words *Camp*

Macaw had been painted on it, but the paint was chipped and fading.

"I hope that means there are macaws here," Violet said. "We saw one kind at the zoo. But I read in my bird guidebook that there are many kinds."

"I suppose so." Nigel shrugged. He turned and led them past the sign to a clearing. Three open-air buildings, each with just one back wall, stood around a fire pit. The buildings had roofs made of dried plants, but there were some gaps where it looked like the plants had blown away. Log benches surrounded the fire pit. A young man was stirring something in a pot over the fire. He had straight black hair under a cap with a circular brim.

"Hello," Henry said to the young man. "I'm Henry, and these are my sisters and brother."

The young man stood up and greeted them. His name was Kwini Macedo.

"Kwini is one of the best guides around," said Nigel. "And a great cook too."

After everyone was introduced, they went to look at the shelters.

"It doesn't look like anyone has been here for some time," Dr. Iris said. "Nigel, I thought you said this was a research camp. It's in very poor shape."

"It was a research camp, but they aren't using it this year," Nigel said. "I assumed someone would have kept it fixed up."

Dr. Iris shook her head. "At least we can sleep on the boat."

"About that…" Nigel's voice trailed off.

Captain Souza walked into the camp. "I don't mean to rush you, but I need to be on my way. I don't want to get behind schedule," he told them.

"What do you mean?" Dr. Iris asked. "What schedule?"

The captain waved back toward the river. "I am sorry, I have to get going. Another group is expecting me upriver."

"I thought *we* hired you," she said. "Why are you going upriver?"

"You did hire me." He pointed a thumb in Nigel's direction. "Or, I should say, Nigel did. To get you here, drop you off, and then pick you up in a few days."

"But we can't stay on shore in these conditions," Dr. Iris said. "These sleeping shelters are falling apart!"

"I'm sorry," the captain said. "The person I'm picking up is going to Manaus for an operation at a hospital. The surgery is already scheduled, and they are counting on me to get them there. If you don't want to stay here, you can come with me, but I must pick up that passenger."

"We can work on the camp and fix it up," Henry said. "All we need are some tools."

"That's right," Jessie added. "We can clear away the dead leaves and cut back the vines that are growing over things."

Dr. Iris walked around the camp one more time before she said anything. She gave a big sigh. "We can stay only if you have tools we can use and there is mosquito netting for all of us," she said to Nigel. "We can't stay here otherwise."

"I do have that," Nigel said. "I got everything on your list."

"I have a few extra tools I can leave you," the captain said.

Dr. Iris looked back toward the river and then at the camp again. "All right. We can stay."

It took the group a long time to unload everything. There were so many supplies, there wasn't much room for their hammocks in the shelters.

"It doesn't look like there is any electricity here to run some of this equipment," Henry said to Nigel. "I don't see a generator."

Nigel shook his head. "I thought they would have left the generator here, but they took it with them."

"Of course they did," said Dr. Iris. "Generators are valuable pieces of equipment."

"But heavy to move," Nigel argued. "I just thought it would have been easier to leave it here. Not to worry, I packed some extra battery packs."

Dr. Iris sighed. Jessie could tell she was frustrated that Nigel wasn't better prepared. Fortunately,

Kwini helped them get everything in order. He showed them how to use vines to tie up the poles that had fallen down and which leaves to use to patch the roofs.

"How did you learn to do all this?" Jessie asked as they worked.

"My father is from this region," Kwini explained. "He was a guide until he retired. I used to go along with him on trips. Now, I do some guide work during the summers when I'm not in college."

It grew dark as they were finishing up. Finally, Nigel said, "Isn't this good enough for tonight? I'm getting hungry."

"Me too!" Benny said.

Kwini, who had been going back and forth between the shelters and a pot simmering over the fire, said, "It's ready when you are!"

"There are plates in one of these crates," Nigel said.

Kwini picked up a stack of large leaves. "We don't need plates. I collected some banana leaves earlier. They work just as well, and we don't have to wash them."

"I like that idea," said Violet.

Kwini ladled out rice and chicken onto a leaf and handed it to Dr. Iris. Then he served the rest of the group.

"It smells delicious!" Jessie said.

Benny took a big bite. "It is delicious!"

Once everyone had eaten and the shelters were repaired, the children relaxed around the fire. The forest around them was filled with the sounds of insects chirping and frogs croaking.

"It's noisy out here," Benny said.

"There must be millions of little creatures, all making noise," Violet added.

"I'm glad I don't hear any big creatures, but they are out there too, aren't they?" Benny asked, glancing around at the darkness surrounding the camp.

"Yes," Nigel said. "The mapinguary is out there, and we're going to find it."

"Dr. Cardoso said you believe the creature is

related to the giant sloth," said Jessie. "Is that right?"

Nigel nodded. "I believe that it may have come from the giant sloth, but it may have changed over time. Who knows what it might be like today?"

"What do you think about the mapinguary, Kwini?" Henry asked.

Kwini shrugged. "I don't know. My father has his own theory though. He thinks his people, the ones who lived here before anyone else, made up the creature for a reason. A hundred years ago, outsiders took over much of this area to get rubber from rubber trees. The people who lived here had to leave or were forced to work for the outsiders. But the outsiders demanded too much work. No one could collect the amount rubber they asked for. The rain forest is a dangerous place. By saying it was even more dangerous, it was a good reason why they couldn't be expected to stay out working when it started to get dark."

Jessie took out her notepad and wrote down what Kwini thought about the creature. She thought it sounded a lot like what their taxi driver had said on the way to the forest.

"I don't believe that at all!" Nigel said. "Those creatures are out there. So many people believe in them, they have to be real. And I'm going to be the one to prove it." He got up. "And I need to film something."

He went into the sleeping shelter and came out a few minutes later carrying one of the camera rigs with the vest. He stood by the fire and began filming himself.

"I'm Nigel Livingstone, and we are here deep in the Amazon jungle, many days away from civilization. We're on the track of the legendary mapinguary, the beast whose mere mention causes fear in anyone who knows of it." He switched the camera to face out away from him. "It's lurking out there, somewhere in the dark." He dropped his voice to a loud whisper. "It might be watching us now." Shutting off the camera, he turned to them and grinned. "What did you think?"

Benny moved closer to Jessie but didn't say anything.

"Don't worry," she told him. "I don't think any creature would want to stand out there in the dark and watch us." She turned to Nigel. "And plus, we aren't really days away from civilization."

"That's right," said Henry. "We saw villages yesterday, and it only took us a day to get here."

Nigel set down his camera equipment. "It makes a better story if viewers think we are a long way from other people."

"Viewers?" Dr. Iris asked.

"I put some of my videos online. Most of them are me reading stories I wrote, but I thought this would be a great chance to record something really exciting."

"You know, Nigel, you said that because many people believe in mapinguaries, they have to be real," Dr. Iris said. "Surely, as a scientist, you know that is not correct. The number of people who believe something doesn't make it true. We'll have to have some real evidence."

"We'll find it," Nigel insisted. "Tomorrow." With that, he went off to the sleeping shelter he was sharing with Kwini.

After a little while, the fire burned down, and the children found their way to their own shelter. As they lay in their hammocks, the noise from the rain forest seemed louder than ever.

"I don't know if I can go to sleep," Benny whispered.

"Me neither." Violet shifted around in her hammock. "I've been thinking about something. Why do you think the scientists who were using this camp didn't come back here this year? Did something scare them away?"

"We can ask Nigel tomorrow," Henry said. "But I wouldn't worry. He and Kwini have been in the Amazon many times."

"It's strange that Nigel has been in the Amazon so many times but doesn't seem prepared," Jessie said. "He brought a solar-powered coffee maker and lots of things that use electricity without knowing if there would be any. It doesn't seem like something a good camper would do."

"I'm going ask him in the morning," Violet said. "There's something strange about all this."

AN EXPEDITION

Jessie awoke to a low growl. It was still dark out, and she was so startled, she sat up to look around. The growling grew louder and louder. Soon everyone was awake.

"What is it?" Benny said. "Is it a mapinguary?"

Nigel dashed down from his hammock and held up a recorder. "It might be!" He circled the camp and then went into the forest. "I'll be back soon," he called.

"Don't get too excited," Kwini said. He got up and went over to the firepit. He raised his voice to be heard over the noise. "It's just howler monkeys."

"That sounds like growling, not howling," Henry said. Everyone climbed out of their hammocks and joined Kwini at the fire.

"I know, but that is the sound they make every morning," Kwini explained. "Each monkey picks a tree where they will spend their day eating leaves. Then they call out to let the other monkeys know the tree is already taken. I guess they don't like to share."

"Really?" Jessie asked. "That's funny."

Kwini smiled. "That's what I've always been told."

"Are they dangerous?" Violet asked.

"No, but they are smart." Kwini added wood to the fire. "My father told me that at one camp he worked at, the monkeys learned how to unzip backpacks. They would sneak into camp and take candy bars. That's why we need to keep the food in sturdy containers."

Kwini opened a box full of kitchen equipment. Jessie went over to see what was inside.

"Was there supposed to be a kitchen at the campsite?" she asked. "That's a lot of cooking supplies."

"I don't think so," said Kwini. "We don't need all these things." He pulled out a round pan with a clasp on the side. When he opened the clasp, the bottom of the pan fell out. "I don't even know what you'd make in this kind of pan."

"It's for cheesecakes," Jessie said. "We aren't going to be making cheesecakes here, are we?"

Kwini laughed. "No, definitely not. I make good pancakes, but I've never tried a cheesecake."

"Can I help with breakfast?" she asked. "I've made pancakes before."

Benny volunteered too.

Kwini held up a wooden spoon. "You can stir, Benny. Jessie, can you get the pancake mix out of that container?"

Jessie went over and opened the container's lid. "Uh-oh." She held up a bag with a hole at the top

76

and a bit of pancake mix at the bottom. "Something got at one of these bags of pancake mix."

Henry looked down at the ground behind her. "There's a trail of it leading into the forest."

Kwini sighed. "Ants. The flour should have been double bagged or put in a metal canister. Ants will chew through bags and carry off what they can. I thought Nigel would have checked that."

Together, they followed the trail of flour to the edge of the clearing. "Here's one of the thieves. Come look."

Benny ran over and crouched down to get a good look. "That's the biggest ant I've ever seen!" he said. He held his hand next to it. "It's as long as my little finger!"

"Yes, they are big, and they bite too," Kwini warned. "It's a very painful bite, so don't get too close. Now, we need to check the rest of the food supplies after breakfast so we don't lose any more."

Nigel came back in time for breakfast. They finished off all the pancakes quickly. After breakfast, they cleaned up. Violet was putting away the pancake mix when a red feather drifted down from above. It landed right by her foot.

"This is pretty!" she said. "I wonder what kind of bird it's from."

Nigel shrugged. "A red bird, I'd say."

"It's from a scarlet macaw," Kwini explained. "I've seen a pair of them a few different times. They must nest close to here. That's probably why the camp is named Camp Macaw."

Now that Nigel was back in the camp, Violet asked the question she had been thinking about the night before. "Nigel, why didn't the scientists come back to Camp Macaw this year? Why did they build these buildings and then leave them? Were they scared of something here?"

"They were on a bird expedition," he replied. "And they ran out of money. That's always the problem with taking expeditions into the Amazon. It takes money, lots of it. If you want someone to fund your trip, you have to have something to show for it. Whatever they found couldn't convince anyone to give them more money to come back. But that's not going to happen to me. My videos are going to convince people to send me back here as many times as I need to find the mapinguary."

He pulled out a backpack from a pile of supplies. "I have a good feeling about today," he said. "I've got something amazing to show you, but to get there, we'll have to take the canoes up a side stream. Let's get organized!"

They brought supplies down to the riverbank and loaded the two canoes.

"I can't believe we get to go in boats made out of logs," Jessie said as she, Violet, and Henry climbed into a canoe with Kwini.

"Do you know how they are made?" Henry asked Kwini.

"Yes, I saw one being made a long time ago," Kwini said. "Once they cut a tree down, they hollow the log out to make the shape of a boat. The last step is to light fire to the inside. That softens the wood enough that it can be widened for people to sit in."

"That's amazing," said Jessie. "I'm glad we get to use them."

"Most people use more modern boats," said Kwini. "But Nigel thought these looked more authentic. The problem is, these are so old, they leak." He pointed to a bucket behind Henry's seat. "If too much water comes in, we may need to bail it out."

Their destination was on a stream off the main river. It was too shallow to use the motors that Nigel and Kwini had used to travel up the river. So the group paddled instead. Trees and vines hung low over the water. They had to duck to avoid getting a branch in the face.

Henry leaned over the edge of the boat. "It's amazing how clear the water is here."

"The way the plants on the sides of the river reflect in the water makes it hard to tell where the water ends and the forest begins," Jessie said.

"Yes, it's like being in a magic land," Violet said.

The trees rustled above them, and then chirping noises filled the air.

"Tamarin monkeys!" Kwini called out. One small monkey climbed down the tree, so that it could look at them.

Benny waved. "Hello, Mr. Tamarin."

"You may be the first human it's ever seen, Benny," said Dr. Iris.

As they continued on, the chirping stopped and was replaced by a loud yipping noise.

Nigel reached forward and pulled a camera out from a backpack, making his boat rock. Dr. Iris and Benny grabbed the sides to steady themselves. "One mapinguary might be calling to another!" Nigel said. "We don't know for sure what kind of noises they make."

"But…doesn't that sound like a toucan?" said Benny.

"I don't know," Nigel said. "There are hundreds of species of birds here. I can't know them all."

"We heard Captain Souza's toucan," Violet said

from the other boat. "It sounded just like that."

"Maybe," Nigel said. "But if we don't see it, we can't know for sure."

Jessie looked back over her shoulder and spoke to Henry in a quiet voice. "I thought Nigel was an expert on birds."

"Yes, it's strange he wouldn't know a toucan call," Henry said.

It took almost two hours before Nigel brought the boat toward shore. "We'll tie it up here," he said.

They climbed out and unloaded the packs. "Kwini and I were here yesterday afternoon, and Kwini marked the trail." Nigel looked around. "I hope you can still find it."

"I can." Kwini got a machete out of the boat and pointed to a plant with a broken stem. "See, there is one of the plants I cut. If you slash them so that the stems do not break in half, it marks the trail," he explained. "It's easy to get lost if you aren't careful, and these plants grow back so fast it doesn't hurt to cut a few."

They hiked up and down several small hills. The ground was slippery with mud and fallen leaves. "I don't know why I thought Brazil was mostly a flat country," Henry said as he reached down to give Benny a hand up a slope.

"I don't either," Jessie said, wiping her face. "It's not easy hiking around here in the heat. But it's amazing to see all the different plants."

It was another hour before Kwini called, "We're almost there!" They followed him to a cleared area full of tree stumps.

"I hope this place is worth it," said Benny.

As the Aldens entered the clearing, Nigel ran ahead. On the other side, there was a hill. At its base was a large, dark opening, which was almost perfectly round.

"Wow, is it a cave?" Benny asked.

"A tunnel," Nigel called.

"It looks like the tunnels that machines make," Henry said when they got close enough to get a good look.

"Except there were never any machines out here," Nigel said. "We believe an animal made this. A big animal."

"Is it still in there?" Violet asked.

CHAPTER 8

IN THE DARK

T here was nothing in there yesterday," Nigel said. "But maybe there is something in there today!"

Dr. Iris put her hand on the side of the entrance. "I've never seen anything like this. But before we arrived, I did some research on giant sloths. There was a mention of the paleoburrows they were thought to have made—ones that look like giant tunnels."

"Paleoburrow? Is that like a burrow a normal animal digs?" Jessie asked.

"Adding *paleo* means that the burrow was built by an extinct creature," Dr. Iris explained.

"So you think this tunnel is thousands of years old?" Violet asked. "Wouldn't it have fallen in?"

"Exactly!" Nigel said. "I think this burrow is much more recent."

"We tried to build a snow tunnel last winter," said Benny. "But it fell in."

"Tunnels have to be made of just the right stuff," Dr. Iris said. "The ground here is very compact."

"Maybe that's why our tunnel didn't work," Benny said.

"That, and Watch jumped on it before it was ready." Henry chuckled.

Benny nodded. "I don't think he likes tunnels."

Jessie looked around the entrance. "How was this tunnel found?" Jessie asked.

Kwini spoke up. "A woman from a bird expedition told Nigel about it. The area had been cleared by illegal loggers. According to the woman, when the loggers found the tunnel, they packed up and left."

"I would too," said Jessie, "if I didn't know about the giant ground sloths."

The group followed Nigel a little farther into the tunnel. It became dark very quickly. Nigel turned on his flashlight.

"What if a mapinguary is hiding in here?" said Benny.

"Or anything else," Violet added. She remembered what Captain Souza had said about being good guests in the rain forest. She didn't think a good guest would walk into an animal's home.

"It makes it more exciting that way!" Nigel called over his shoulder.

He turned on a camera attached to his vest and began to move down the tunnel. "It is believed these amazing structures were made by giant sloths," he said for the camera, "but there is no way of dating them. They may very well have been made more recently by the ferocious mapinguary that roams the forest. We have to go quietly."

Dr. Iris, Kwini, and the children followed at a

distance. "I disagree with Nigel," Dr. Iris said. "I do think it is a paleoburrow and was made a very long time ago. I think we are fine to go farther in."

They all switched on their flashlights and followed after Nigel. The tunnel was so large no one had to duck their heads.

"We think it goes several hundred feet into the hill," Nigel said from up ahead.

Henry's fingers brushed the wall as he walked. There were rough ridges carved into the wall.

"The ridges are a clue," said Dr. Iris. "Scientists think they were made by an animal with large claws scraping the soil away. The ridges would then be the spaces between the claws."

"The claws on the giant sloth skeleton were long enough and big enough to be able to dig," Jessie said.

"So were the ones on that scary statue," Violet added.

Henry stopped and looked around. "But when you dig a long tunnel, you have to put the soil somewhere," he said. "How would an animal carry it all out of here?"

"A very good question," said Dr. Iris. "They would have to keep scooping it backward as they backed out of the tunnel. It would be a tremendous amount of work."

"They must have figured out a way," Jessie said. "I've seen pictures of how prairie dogs have a whole network of tunnels."

"This would be one big prairie dog," said Benny.

The group continued down the tunnel. Nigel was so far ahead they could see only his silhouette and the light from his flashlight bobbing up and down.

"I don't hear anything," Benny said. "That means there is probably nothing in here, right?"

"Right," Jessie said. "I think we are safe."

Suddenly, Nigel stopped narrating for the camera ahead, and his light swept back and forth across the tunnel. "I think there's something here!" he called.

The next thing the Aldens knew, Nigel's light went out, and he let out a shriek.

Dr. Iris took off running toward him, and the

children followed with Kwini. When they reached him, they shined their flashlights around the tunnel. They had reached the end. "Nigel, there's nothing here," Dr. Iris said. "Are you hurt?"

There was silence for a moment. Then Nigel said, "Why did you have to say that? I was making a good video!"

"We thought you were in trouble," said Jessie.

"No, no. But now I need to do another take. Everything was going so well too!"

The group walked out of the tunnel. When they got to the entrance, Nigel turned on his camera and began again. "It is believed these amazing structures were made by giant sloths, but they have been made by the ferocious mapinguary that roams the forest. There may be one inside…"

"Why is he saying that?" Benny asked. "He knows there isn't anything in the tunnel. We walked all the way to the end."

"He's just pretending for the film," Henry said.

"That doesn't seem right," said Violet.

Dr. Iris shook her head. "No, but it's very common, I'm afraid. Often what you see on television is staged to make something seem more frightening than it really is."

"Not your program though," said Violet. "Right?"

Dr. Iris shook her head. "Our show is to learn about the legends and examine the evidence."

"Is there any evidence to prove the tunnel was made by giant sloths?" Jessie asked.

"That is a very good question," Dr. Iris said. "It would be very difficult to say."

"What if someone found a skeleton in one?" Benny asked.

"Or a fossil claw stuck in the wall?" Violet suggested.

"A skeleton or a fossil claw found like that would be excellent proof," Dr. Iris said. "But the conditions in the rain forest aren't right to turn something into a fossil. Remember, the best way a bone becomes a fossil is when it is covered up with dirt. A claw stuck in a tunnel wall like this would just break down and disappear."

Henry looked at one of the walls near the entrance. "That's too bad," he said. "It really does seem like an animal made this tunnel. I wish we could find some real evidence."

The children were quiet for a moment. Then Jessie spoke up. "We did find evidence in one way," she said. "No matter what made this tunnel, we learned that the legend of the mapinguary kept the loggers away."

"Excellent point," said Dr. Iris. "Yes, the power of stories can be very strong. I have a feeling that will be an important part of our research."

———

The trip back seemed to take longer than it had to get to the tunnel. It was almost dusk by the time they tied the boats up. As they ate dinner around the campfire, the Aldens were happy to relax after a long day of travel.

However, Nigel was restless. He walked around the camp with night-vision goggles, looking for footprints. "Take a look at this beauty!" he called.

Everyone hurried over, and Nigel pointed down to a large leaf.

Violet got close enough to see and then jerked back. "Is that a big spider?"

"It is!" Nigel said. "It's a pink-toed tarantula. Isn't it fantastic? Look at its toes. They really are pink. I used to want a tarantula as a pet, but my father hates spiders."

"Aren't they dangerous?" Jessie asked.

"Not if you are careful," Nigel said. "They can even be held if you don't startle them."

"I thought…" Henry began. "Professor Cardoso said you hate spiders."

Nigel frowned. "No, I don't hate spiders. He must be confused. I'm going to get my camera and film this. It will go great with the bits about the dangers of the Amazon."

After Nigel was done filming, he got out his audio

recording device. It contained the audio recording he had sent to Dr. Iris early in the trip. "I'm going to play it, and maybe one will answer back." He played the roaring noise, and everyone sat quietly and listened for a response.

"I just hear the regular sounds," Violet said finally. She was relieved nothing had roared back.

"Nigel, I've been wondering, where did you get the recording?" Dr. Iris asked.

"A man in Manaus," Nigel replied. "People there know I'm looking for the mapinguary and that I'll pay for good information. The man came to me with the recording and the location where he heard it. He swore he'd never heard anything like it before."

"It could be a jaguar," said Dr. Iris. "Did you compare the sound you have to the sound of a jaguar roaring?"

"No, the man who gave it to me knows this area," Nigel said. "He wouldn't claim it was a mapinguary if he knew it was a jaguar."

"Maybe he just wanted to be paid," Kwini suggested.

"It's too bad we can't get a signal on a cell phone," Henry said. "It would be easy to find a recording of a jaguar on the Internet."

Nigel put the equipment away. "Well, we can't. I'll try again tomorrow night. I have something else I need to work on." He got out one of the laptops he had brought. "Want to help me with a ghost story I recorded? I put a new one up on the Internet every month, and I'm going to need to upload this one as soon as I get back to Manaus to keep on schedule."

"What do you want us to do?" Violet asked.

"I need some sound effects. I tell the stories, but then I add in extra touches. Here, I'll show you what I mean."

They listened to a spooky story about a haunted house that had sound effects added in.

"Did you write that story?" Jessie asked. "It's really good and scary."

"I did, and I'm glad you thought it was scary,"

Nigel said. "The one I'm working on now is about a family of ghosts."

The children agreed to help Nigel make sound effects for his story. Henry and Jessie played the parts of the older ghosts, and Violet and Benny played the parts of the two younger ghosts. When they were done, the children laughed as they went into their shelter to go to sleep for the night. Making sound effects was a fun distraction from thinking about scary monsters.

But as Henry laid in his hammock, he wondered: Why was a scientist so interested in making stories?

CHAPTER 9

A CLOSE CALL

The next morning, Nigel was up first. By the time they had all finished eating, he was ready to go. "We're going to hike to our site today. I think it's a perfect spot for a mapinguary to live," he told them. "Even if we don't see one, we might find footprints!"

Dr. Iris helped pack up the right supplies, and they started to hike on an old trail through the rain forest. They had traveled almost two hours before Henry spotted something unusual. The path appeared to end at a wall of vines.

"Is that a building up ahead?" he asked. "I can see stone blocks underneath the vines."

"Yes," Kwini said as they drew closer. "There must have been a town here a long time ago."

"This is it!" Nigel said.

At the end of the wall, the path turned into an overgrown street. Small trees sprouted between paving stones, and vines trailed across it. Nigel went down the street and spent time filming the area.

"What is this place?" Jessie asked.

Parts of buildings, mostly collapsed, lined both sides of the street. The roofs of the buildings were gone. Plants and trees were growing out of the floors.

"I do not know its name," Kwini said. "But there are abandoned towns like this in many places in the Amazon."

"It's strange to think people abandon whole towns," Henry said.

"They were built when farming for rubber was

legal here," said Kwini. "After farmers started growing rubber trees in other parts of the world, people slowly moved out of towns like these."

"I thought more of the buildings would be intact," Nigel said, filming as he went. "An old building would be a perfect lair for a mapinguary."

"The trees grow quickly here," said Dr. Iris. She scanned the old buildings. Some of the trees were quite tall. "I would guess that this town has been abandoned for at least ten years."

"It's closer to five," said Kwini.

"Wow," said Jessie. "That's amazing."

Dr. Iris reached out and grabbed a branch extending through an empty window. "Remember how we talked about how everything in the rain forest changes over time?" she said.

Jessie nodded.

"The plants and trees do too," she said. "Every plant in the forest has adapted to grow quickly. If it doesn't, it will be overtaken by those that do, and it will not receive the water and sunlight it needs.

That's one of the reasons things grow so quickly here."

"So each plant is like a master grower," said Benny.

Dr. Iris smiled. "That's one way of putting it."

Violet looked at the beautiful plants growing in the old town. She liked the idea of the rain forest growing back after people were gone.

After a few minutes, Nigel returned to the group.

"I want to look for footprints behind the buildings," he said. "It's possible mapinguaries do come here. Maybe they are waiting for the humans to come back! I need to record that idea."

He went back to recording himself talking about mapinguary lairs and humans walking into danger. When he was finished, he moved to the back of the buildings.

Benny looked around the abandoned town. "His video is going to be scary! What if one really is waiting here?"

"This village has been abandoned for a long time," said Henry. "Even if there was a creature, it wouldn't wait around for someone to show up. But it is a spooky idea."

"I found a footprint!" Nigel called.

The group hurried around a building to where Nigel was pointing at the ground. There was a mark in the soil that looked like no footprint the Aldens had ever seen before. At the back there was a deep print that looked like a heel mark and four long prints that looked like claws.

"Maybe someone created it," said Violet. "Like the bigfoot prints we found that were made-up."

Everyone turned to Nigel.

"Hey, don't look at me!" he said. "I didn't have the time to make this."

It was true: unless Nigel had created the footprint some other time, there was no way he could have made it.

Kwini looked around. "I don't recognize this footprint," he said. "But I can tell that it's fresh."

"What do you think, Dr. Iris?" Henry asked.

She bent down to examine it. "I'm not familiar

enough with the rain forest to tell. It could be a footprint, or it could have been caused by something else, like an animal stepping on a branch."

Nigel scouted the area and then called out, "This might be another one! I need to take a cast of both of these."

"A cast?" Violet asked. "What does that mean?"

"A cast is a way of taking a record of a footprint," said Dr. Iris.

Nigel set down his backpack and pulled out a bag of white powder. "Kwini, can I have some water? The instructions say to cut the top off the bag and pour the water in, then mix it around."

"It's much easier to mix in a bucket," Dr. Iris said. "I've taken hundreds of casts, if you'd like me to do the mixing. I can get the consistency just right."

"All right." Nigel handed over the supplies to Dr. Iris.

"You need to get the water out of the impression first," she said. "Clear all the leaves and twigs out of it. Then use the paper towels to soak up the water."

When the powder was mixed, she said, "It's tempting to pour a lot in the center and let it spread out, but that can change the shape. We'll pour it slowly around the edges and it will fill in." She did so, then she pulled out a ruler from her pack. "Now, we smooth it down so no air bubbles remain. It will take a while to dry. We'll have to leave them here and come back."

"That's okay. We can look around some more," Nigel said.

While the casts were drying, the group explored the area. They hadn't gone far when Nigel stopped. He grabbed Kwini's arm. "I saw something move! Let's follow it!"

"Wait," Kwini said. "We can't just run after it. If there is an animal out there, it will run away."

"Whatever it is, it probably knows we are here already," Jessie said. "Almost all animals can smell better than humans."

"I think *I* smell something," said Violet, scrunching up her face. "And whatever it is, it's not good."

"We have to follow it," Nigel said. "No one will believe me unless I get something on film. Kwini, get out the net, and Henry, be ready. The two of you run around the creature, one on either side until its trapped in the net. I'll film it all."

Kwini and Henry looked at each other. Kwini shrugged and then got out the net, handing one side of it to Henry.

"You don't really think you can catch whatever it is!" Dr. Iris said to Nigel.

"We can try," Nigel said. "It's why we are here, after all."

"We're here to see how the legend could have come about, not to actually try to capture a large animal!" Dr. Iris said.

Nigel ignored her and switched on the camera. He held up his hand for everyone to be quiet. "We're here, deep in the Amazon jungle," he said into the camera, "on the trail of what may be the amazing discovery of the century! An actual monster of the Amazon, the legendary mapinguary is a creature so fearsome that people who live here tremble at its mere mention."

He motioned for everyone to move forward as he began to walk. After a few minutes, they came to a clearing. Nigel motioned for everyone to stop. Ahead, a large, hairy creature was hunched over something on the ground. The creature reared up and put its front legs on the tree. Then it turned its head toward them.

Benny grabbed onto Jessie's hand. Violet clapped her hand over her mouth.

"Back up," Kwini said. "It's not going to attack us. It's just warning us off."

But instead of letting out a roar, the creature let out a small squeak. Then it put its front paws back onto the ground and waddled off into the forest.

"Did you see its long snout?" Jessie said. "That was definitely *not* a monster."

"It was an anteater!" said Benny. "We saw one at the zoo!"

Henry chuckled. "That explains the smell. I read

in my guidebook that anteaters are like skunks. They mark their territory. The scent scares off predators."

Violet plugged her nose. "I can see why."

The children laughed. Everyone was relieved that it was not really the monster from the stories. Dr. Iris led them to the tree where the anteater had been. At the base, a stream of ants was going in and out under a large root.

"That anteater really is a master eater," said Benny. "I never would have thought there were so many ants in there."

After they were done looking around the clearing, Nigel headed back to the abandoned town to check on his footprints. The rest of the group took their time. On the way, Henry said, "Didn't Professor Cardoso say that the giant ground sloths went extinct because of humans?"

Dr. Iris nodded. "That is the theory, yes."

"Well, I've been thinking," Henry continued. "You said that everything that lives in the rain forest has changed over a long time so it can live here."

"Like the anteater's snout," said Benny. He listed off the other animals they had seen. "And the tree sloth's disguise. And the toucan's call."

"And the fast-growing trees," Jessie added.

"So if the ground sloth really did survive," said Henry. "It would have had to adapt too. To avoid going extinct."

Jessie nodded. She could see what her brother was saying. "If the giant sloth survived, it would have to become an expert too: an expert at staying away from humans."

"That is a very interesting theory," Dr. Iris said. She added, "And it's possible that having a strong smell could help keep humans away."

"But that is different from the story of the monster," said Violet. "According to the story, the creature chases people away. It doesn't hide from them."

"Another good observation," said Dr. Iris. "It seems like the two are describing different things."

When the children caught up to Nigel, he was

filming the plaster casts they had created. He'd wiped dirt on his face to make himself look like he had been on a chase through the forest.

"The creature got away," he said into the camera, "despite all our efforts to catch it. Whatever it was, it was fearsome. The smell of it alone was nearly overwhelming. Luckily, we found some evidence."

After Nigel turned off his camera, Benny said, "I really think you are cheating. Some people are going to watch that and think you didn't know it was an anteater."

Nigel shrugged. "That part might not be real, but these footprints are."

"We don't know that," Jessie pointed out. "We don't know what made them."

They turned to Dr. Iris, and she nodded. But Nigel just shook his head. He huffed and started back down the trail.

When the group arrived at camp, everyone was hot and tired. But Nigel seemed to be in a better mood. "I think I'll go for a swim before dinner," he said.

"You can," said Kwini. "But I should check to see if it's safe."

"How do you know if it's safe?" Violet asked.

"I'll show you. Let's go down to the dock." They followed Kwini and Nigel to the river. Midway across, they could see dolphins coming to the surface for air.

Kwini pointed. "See the dolphins? If they are here, there are no caiman in the area, and it's safe to swim."

Nigel took off his shoes and jumped into the water. He swam out away from shore, and the dolphins darted about, leaping out of the water.

"They are having fun!" Benny said.

For a few minutes, the dolphins swam around as Nigel treaded water. "Come on in!" he said. "The water feels great!"

Violet looked around. She couldn't see the dolphins anymore.

Kwini had noticed too. "Nigel, you'd better come in," he said.

"Why? I don't see anything," Nigel called back.

Kwini stood up. He pointed across the river to the other bank. "I see a caiman!"

Nigel swam for the shore and scrambled onto the dock just as a caiman appeared on the near side of the river. Then everyone hurried away from the river and up to camp.

When they were seated safely around the campfire, Benny said to Nigel, "Professor Cardoso said you got bit by a caiman. That must have been scary."

"And really hurt," Violet said.

Nigel didn't say anything for a moment. Then he shook his head. "Not me. He really must have me confused with someone else."

Henry and Jessie shared a suspicious look.

"I suppose he does," Henry said. "But he acted like he knew you well. He mentioned you had trouble walking, and I'm sure you'd have some sort of scar from an attack."

Nigel stuck his legs out. "See? No scars. But I do wish I would have filmed that." He went and got his camera. "Maybe the big guy is still down by the water. I'll try to get some footage. Kwini, would you come along and tell me if you spot him?"

After the two had gone down to the riverbank, Dr. Iris said, "That was quite exciting, maybe a little too exciting. If everyone is all right, I need to catch up on my notes."

"We're fine," Henry said, but as soon as Dr. Iris had gone to her shelter, he turned to his siblings. "There is something strange about Nigel."

"I'd say," said Benny. "Who would want to swim when there are caimans around?"

"I don't mean that," Henry said. "I mean he doesn't seem to be anything like the person Professor Cardoso told us about."

Violet nodded. "He doesn't recognize the calls of toucans and macaws, but he wrote a whole book about birds in the Amazon."

"Can I see the bird book?" Henry asked.

Violet gave him her guidebook, and he opened to the first pages.

"What is even weirder is the date this book was published," he said. "More than twenty years ago. I don't know how old Nigel is, but he doesn't look that old. He couldn't have published a book when he was our age."

"If Nigel isn't the Nigel Livingstone who wrote this book, than who is he?" asked Violet.

"I don't know," said Jessie. "But I think Henry is right. We should show this book to Dr. Iris."

The Aldens found Dr. Iris lying in her hammock and writing in her journal.

"We think something is strange about Nigel," Henry said. "He doesn't really seem to be a bird expert." He explained about the date in the book and showed it to Dr. Iris.

While she was looking at it, Jessie listed all the other odd things they had noticed. "Nigel doesn't shave his head, like Professor Cardoso said. He doesn't have any scars on his leg where the caiman bit him. He doesn't walk with a limp."

"And he's not scared of spiders!" Violet added.

Dr. Iris sat up in her hammock. "Very interesting," she said. "Of course, I have noticed that Nigel is different from what I thought he would be, but I hadn't thought that he might be a different person. I'm going to ask him as soon as he gets back."

"He'll probably just make up a story," said Benny. "Like he's been doing when he's filming."

Benny's words gave Henry an idea. "He is very good at making up stories, isn't he?" Henry snapped his fingers. "I think I know who he is."

REVEALED

Before Henry had a chance to explain, Nigel and Kwini returned to camp. Dr. Iris held up the guidebook on birds as she approached him. "This book was published twenty years ago. You are far too young to have written it, and you are certainly not an expert on Amazon expeditions. I think it's time to tell us who you really are."

Nigel looked at the book and then down at the ground.

"Is the real Nigel Livingstone your father?" Henry asked.

"What?" Dr. Iris asked.

"You're right, Henry!" Jessie said. "Professor Cardoso told us Nigel Livingstone had a son, and the son loved stories ever since he was a little boy."

"He said that the son was going to help him record a story too," said Violet. "Is that you?"

Nigel looked back at them. At first, it looked like he might argue. Then he sighed. "You're right. I did not write the book. But my name really is Nigel Livingstone. I have the same name as my father. He's the man who is the expert."

"I don't understand," Dr. Iris said. "I'm sure I had the correct email address for Nigel Livingstone, the scientist."

"You did," said Nigel. "My father isn't in good health, and I read and answer his emails. When I saw your email, I thought it was the perfect chance for me. I've been wanting to go on an expedition for a long time to search for the mapinguary, but I

couldn't raise the money. I thought it would help my father too. When he published his theory about the giant ground sloths still being alive, it really hurt his reputation. I thought if I found proof of some kind, it would help him."

"You shouldn't trick people," Benny said.

"I know," said Nigel. "But I didn't think it would do any harm."

"We trusted that you would be an experienced Amazon explorer," Dr. Iris said. "I'm not sure what we would have done without Kwini. This trip could have been a disaster."

"I'm really, really sorry," Nigel said.

Dr. Iris sighed. "I suppose since everything turned out all right, we can let this go, but you have to promise not to pretend to be your father. Or anyone else."

"I promise," Nigel said, sitting down on a log.

"And if you want to help your father, you shouldn't post your video about the mapinguary online," said Henry. "That will only hurt his case."

Dr. Iris nodded. "That's a good point, Henry. The

best way to help is not to mislead people but to find real evidence."

Nigel put his head in his hands. "How can I do that?"

The others sat down around the fire. "I think you've already started," said Dr. Iris. "The tunnel we saw is very interesting. And the footprints you found are as well. With your father's help, I imagine people would be happy to fund another expedition. Finding good evidence takes time. It doesn't happen on a single trip."

Nigel nodded. The children could tell that he really did want to help his father. They hoped that Nigel's next trip would help him do that.

Dr. Iris looked at her watch. "It's been a long day. Tomorrow morning we need to pack up so we are ready to leave when the boat comes back. Since the other passenger is on the way to a hospital, the captain won't want any delays."

The next day, the camp was all packed up by lunchtime. The Aldens sat on the dock, but there was no sign of Captain Souza and his boat.

"What if river pirates got him?" Benny asked. "They might have stolen his boat."

"He wouldn't be going anywhere where there are pirates," Kwini said. "He is a very experienced boat captain. I'm sure there is a good explanation."

"There it is!" said Violet.

The *Toucan* came chugging toward them. As it pulled up to the dock, they heard Figly yipping from the pilothouse.

"Sorry I'm a bit late," the captain called.

"We were afraid pirates had taken your boat," Benny said.

The captain smiled. "No pirates. We had some engine trouble, but it's all fixed."

"We're ready to go, but it will take a bit of time to get everything loaded," Dr. Iris said. "How is your other passenger?"

"He's all right. He's sleeping now. I'll get the other

122

crew members to help load."

Once the boat was loaded, everyone said their good-byes. Nigel and Kwini waved at them from the dock as the boat pulled away. The two were going to take the canoes back to Manaus later that day. The Aldens stood at the railing watching the camp disappear from view. Behind the boat, two dolphins darted back and forth and then swam back toward the camp.

"Good-bye, Mr. and Mrs. Dolphin!" Benny called.

The children laughed, and then they were quiet for a while as the scenery went by.

Dr. Iris asked, "What do you think? Are giant sloths somewhere out there?"

"I think the tunnel that Nigel showed us was amazing," said Violet.

"Those footprints were cool too," said Benny.

"I think there might be something unknown out there," said Jessie. "But Nigel and his father's story needs more evidence."

"I hope he finds it," said Benny.

"And what about the legend of our rain forest monster?" asked Dr. Iris.

"I don't think the mapinguary is real," said Henry. "But the story is still alive."

"And it's doing some good," said Jessie. "It helped keep our taxi driver from wandering into the wilderness when he was a boy."

"And it might have helped scare away those illegal loggers," said Violet.

Henry looked at the toucan, Figly, with his long, colorful beak. "It's like the other things we learned about in the rain forest," he said. "The story has changed over time. It might have started as a story about the giant sloths, a long time ago, but I think it became a story to remind people to do the right thing."

Violet nodded. "Good stories find a way to stick around."

Dr. Iris looked at the four children proudly. "I think that is the perfect way to end our show," she said. "You all have helped me so much this summer. I can't thank you enough."

The children looked out at the rain forest as it passed by. "I miss being home with Grandfather and Watch," said Benny. "But I'm going to miss investigating stories too."

"I'm sure you'll find more stories to investigate soon," said Dr. Iris.

Jessie put her hand on Benny's shoulder. "We always do."

THE BOXCAR CHILDREN

GREAT ADVENTURE

An Exciting 5-Book Miniseries

**Henry, Jessie, Violet, and Benny Alden
are on a secret mission that takes
them around the world.**

When Violet finds a turtle statue that nobody's seen
before in an old trunk at home, the children are on the
case. The clue turns out to be an invitation to the
Reddimus Society, a secret guild dedicated to returning
lost treasures to where they belong.

Now the Aldens must take the statue and six mysterious
boxes across the country to deliver them safely—and keep
them out of the hands of the Reddimus Society's enemies.
It's just the beginning of
the Boxcar Children's
most amazing
adventure yet.

Check out The Boxcar Children® Interactive Mysteries!

Have you ever wanted to help the Aldens crack a case? Now you can with these interactive, choose-your-own-path-style mysteries.

978-0-8075-2850-1 · US $6.99

978-0-8075-2860-0 · US $6.99

978-0-8075-2862-4 · US $6.99

978-0-8075-2857-0 · US $6.99

Add to Your
Boxcar Children Collection
with New Books and Sets!

The first sixteen books are now available in
four individual boxed sets.

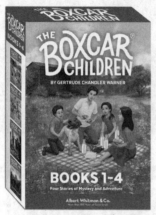

978-0-8075-0854-1 · US $24.99

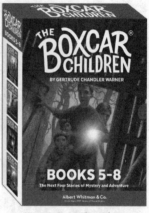

978-0-8075-0857-2 · US $24.99

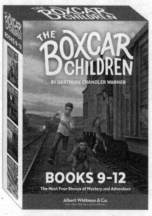

978-0-8075-0840-4 · US $24.99

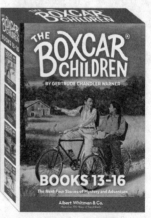

978-0-8075-0834-3 · US $24.99

Look out for
The Boxcar Children® DVDs!

The Boxcar Children and *Surprise Island* animated movie adaptations are both available on DVD, featuring Martin Sheen and J.K. Simmons.

Introducing The Boxcar Children®
Educational Augmented Reality App

Watch and listen to your favorite Alden characters as they spring from the pages to act out scenes, ask questions, and encourage a love of reading. The app works with any paperback or hardcover copy of *The Boxcar Children*, the first book in the series, printed after 1942.

NEW!
The Boxcar Children®
DVD and Book Set

This set includes Gertrude Chandler Warner's classic chapter book in paperback as well as the animated movie adaptation featuring Martin Sheen, J.K. Simmons, Joey King, Jadon Sand, Mackenzie Foy, and Zachary Gordon.

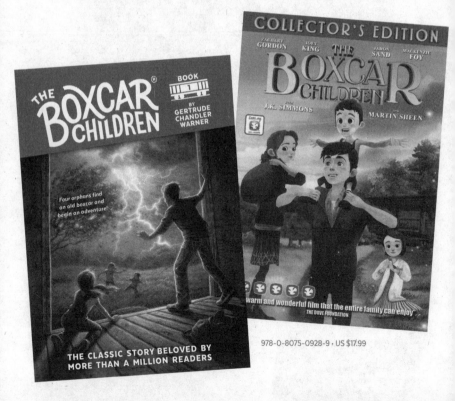

978-0-8075-0928-9 · US $17.99

The Boxcar Children, Fully Illustrated

This fully illustrated edition celebrates Gertrude Chandler Warner's timeless story. Featuring all-new full-color artwork as well as an afterword about the author, the history of the book, and The Boxcar Children® legacy, this volume will be treasured by first-time readers and longtime fans alike.

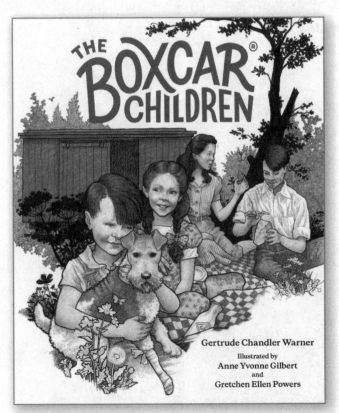

Gertrude Chandler Warner

Illustrated by
Anne Yvonne Gilbert
and
Gretchen Ellen Powers

978-0-8075-0925-8 · US $34.99

Introducing The Boxcar Children® Early Readers

Adapted from the beloved chapter books, these new early readers allow kids to begin reading with the stories that started it all.

THE BOXCAR CHILDREN
Based on the book by Gertrude Chandler Warner

HC 978-0-8075-0839-8 · US $12.99
PB 978-0-8075-0835-0 · US $4.99

SURPRISE ISLAND
Based on the movie *Surprise Island*
Based on the book by Gertrude Chandler Warner

HC 978-0-8075-7675-5 · US $12.99
PB 978-0-8075-7679-3 · US $4.99

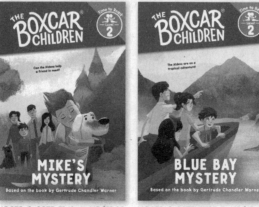

MIKE'S MYSTERY
Based on the book by Gertrude Chandler Warner

HC 978-0-8075-5142-4 · US $12.99
PB 978-0-8075-5139-4 · US $4.99

BLUE BAY MYSTERY
Based on the book by Gertrude Chandler Warner

HC 978-0-8075-0795-7 · US $12.99
PB 978-0-8075-0800-8 · US $4.99

HC 978-0-8075-9367-7 · US $12.99
PB 978-0-8075-9370-7 · US $4.99

HC 978-0-8075-5402-9 · US $12.99
PB 978-0-8075-5435-7 · US $4.99

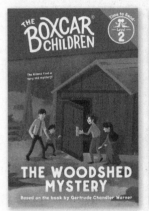

HC 978-0-8075-9210-6 · US $12.99
PB 978-0-8075-9216-8 · US $4.99

HC 978-0-8075-4548-5 · US $12.99
PB 978-0-8075-4552-2 · US $4.99

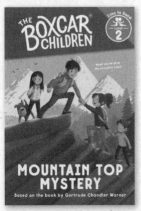

HC 978-0-8075-5291-9 · US $12.99
PB 978-0-8075-5289-6 · US $4.99

THE BOXCAR CHILDREN® MYSTERIES

THE MYSTERY OF THE WILD PONIES

THE MYSTERY IN THE COMPUTER GAME

THE HONEYBEE MYSTERY

THE MYSTERY AT THE CROOKED HOUSE

THE HOCKEY MYSTERY

THE MYSTERY OF THE MIDNIGHT DOG

THE MYSTERY OF THE SCREECH OWL

THE SUMMER CAMP MYSTERY

THE COPYCAT MYSTERY

THE HAUNTED CLOCK TOWER MYSTERY

THE MYSTERY OF THE TIGER'S EYE

THE DISAPPEARING STAIRCASE MYSTERY

THE MYSTERY ON BLIZZARD MOUNTAIN

THE MYSTERY OF THE SPIDER'S CLUE

THE CANDY FACTORY MYSTERY

THE MYSTERY OF THE MUMMY'S CURSE

THE MYSTERY OF THE STAR RUBY

THE STUFFED BEAR MYSTERY

THE MYSTERY OF ALLIGATOR SWAMP

THE MYSTERY AT SKELETON POINT

THE TATTLETALE MYSTERY

THE COMIC BOOK MYSTERY

THE GREAT SHARK MYSTERY

THE ICE CREAM MYSTERY

THE MIDNIGHT MYSTERY

THE MYSTERY IN THE FORTUNE COOKIE

THE BLACK WIDOW SPIDER MYSTERY

THE RADIO MYSTERY

THE MYSTERY OF THE RUNAWAY GHOST

THE FINDERS KEEPERS MYSTERY

THE MYSTERY OF THE HAUNTED BOXCAR

THE CLUE IN THE CORN MAZE

THE GHOST OF THE CHATTERING BONES

THE SWORD OF THE SILVER KNIGHT

THE GAME STORE MYSTERY

THE MYSTERY OF THE ORPHAN TRAIN

THE VANISHING PASSENGER

THE GIANT YO-YO MYSTERY

THE CREATURE IN OGOPOGO LAKE

THE ROCK 'N' ROLL MYSTERY

THE SECRET OF THE MASK

THE SEATTLE PUZZLE

THE GHOST IN THE FIRST ROW

THE BOX THAT WATCH FOUND

A HORSE NAMED DRAGON

THE GREAT DETECTIVE RACE

THE GHOST AT THE DRIVE-IN MOVIE

THE MYSTERY OF THE TRAVELING TOMATOES

THE SPY GAME

THE DOG-GONE MYSTERY

THE VAMPIRE MYSTERY

SUPERSTAR WATCH

THE SPY IN THE BLEACHERS

THE AMAZING MYSTERY SHOW

THE PUMPKIN HEAD MYSTERY

THE CUPCAKE CAPER

THE CLUE IN THE RECYCLING BIN

MONKEY TROUBLE

THE ZOMBIE PROJECT

THE GREAT TURKEY HEIST

THE GARDEN THIEF

THE BOARDWALK MYSTERY

THE MYSTERY OF THE FALLEN TREASURE

THE RETURN OF THE GRAVEYARD GHOST

THE MYSTERY OF THE STOLEN SNOWBOARD

THE MYSTERY OF THE WILD WEST BANDIT

THE MYSTERY OF THE SOCCER SNITCH

THE MYSTERY OF THE GRINNING GARGOYLE

THE MYSTERY OF THE MISSING POP IDOL

THE MYSTERY OF THE STOLEN DINOSAUR BONES

THE MYSTERY AT THE CALGARY STAMPEDE

THE SLEEPY HOLLOW MYSTERY

THE LEGEND OF THE IRISH CASTLE

THE CELEBRITY CAT CAPER

HIDDEN IN THE HAUNTED SCHOOL

THE ELECTION DAY DILEMMA

THE DOUGHNUT WHODUNIT

THE ROBOT RANSOM

THE LEGEND OF THE HOWLING WEREWOLF

THE DAY OF THE DEAD MYSTERY

THE HUNDRED-YEAR MYSTERY

THE SEA TURTLE MYSTERY

SECRET ON THE THIRTEENTH FLOOR

THE POWER DOWN MYSTERY

MYSTERY AT CAMP SURVIVAL

THE MYSTERY OF THE FORGOTTEN FAMILY

THE SKELETON KEY MYSTERY

SCIENCE FAIR SABOTAGE

NEW! THE GREAT GREENFIELD BAKE-OFF

NEW! THE BEEKEEPER MYSTERY

GERTRUDE CHANDLER WARNER discovered when she was teaching that many readers who like an exciting story could find no books that were both easy and fun to read. She decided to try to meet this need, and her first book, *The Boxcar Children*, quickly proved she had succeeded.

Miss Warner drew on her own experiences to write the mystery. As a child she spent hours watching trains go by on the tracks opposite her family home. She often dreamed about what it would be like to set up housekeeping in a caboose or freight car—the situation the Alden children find themselves in.

While the mystery element is central to each of Miss Warner's books, she never thought of them as strictly juvenile mysteries. She liked to stress the Aldens' independence and resourcefulness and their solid New England devotion to using up and making do. The Aldens go about most of their adventures with as little adult supervision as possible—something else that delights young readers.

Miss Warner lived in Putnam, Connecticut, until her death in 1979. During her lifetime, she received hundreds of letters from girls and boys telling her how much they liked her books.